Disney's
CLASSIC MICKEY

VOLUME 1

EYENOVELS

A Welcome/Ocular Book

DISNEY
EDITIONS

Eyenovels™ are coproduced by Welcome Enterprises, Inc. and Ocular Books
Eyenovels™ logo design by Gregory Wakabayashi

Conceived by Roger Warner

Edited and designed by Roger Warner, H. Clark Wakabayashi, and Jon Glick

Additional design by Michelle DiLisio
Production assistance by Elizabeth Kessler

For Disney Editions, Editorial by
Ken Geist, Wendy Lefkon, Rich Thomas

The producers would like to thank the following people for their support:

Dave Smith, The Walt Disney Archives
Ed Squair, The Walt Disney Photo Library
Mark Reinhart, Lasting Impressions

Library of Congress Cataloging-in-Publication on file.

FIRST EDITION
Printed in The United States of America
1 3 5 7 9 10 8 6 4 2

Brave Little Tailor

Premiere Date: September 23, 1938

In his films, Mickey Mouse appears in various times and places, but his underlying character stays the same. He is the underdog (or is it undermouse?) who gets himself in improbable situations that require courage, resourcefulness, and lots of physical comedy to get back out again. In this short classic, nominated for an Academy Award®, a misunderstanding gets the plot rolling. Mickey, a humble tailor, must defeat a MUCH bigger man to win the hand of the Princess Minnie.

A LONG TIME AGO, A TINY LITTLE KINGDOM HAD A GREAT BIG PROBLEM—AND NOBODY KNEW HOW TO FIX IT!

ON A QUIET SIDE STREET LIVED A FRIENDLY TAILOR WHO KNEW NOTHING OF THE KINGDOM'S BIG CRISIS.

HE WAS A HAPPY LAD—EXCEPT FOR SOME PESKY FLIES!

OH BOY, SEVEN!

THE TAILOR WAS VERY HAPPY AS HE COUNTED HIS CATCH.

MEANWHILE, ON THE STREET OUTSIDE HIS WINDOW . . .

Say, did YOU ever kill a GIANT?

I KILLED SEVEN WITH ONE BLOW!

SEVEN???

He killed SEVEN giants with one blow!

SEVEN WITH ONE BLOW?

How many?

Six?

SEVEN!

RUMOR OF THE TAILOR'S AMAZING STRENGTH QUICKLY SPREAD THROUGHOUT THE ENTIRE TOWN.

SEVEN!!!

Jiminy Cricket!

Who?

The tailor?

WITH ONE BLOW!!!

SEVEN GIANTS WITH ONE BLOW!

SEVEN!?!

EVEN THE SOLDIERS OUTSIDE THE CASTLE HEARD THE NEWS.

A GUARD RUSHED TO THE THRONE ROOM, WHERE THE KING AND HIS LOVELY DAUGHTER SAT LOOKING VERY SAD.

ASTONISHED AT WHAT HE'D HEARD, THE KING ROARED:

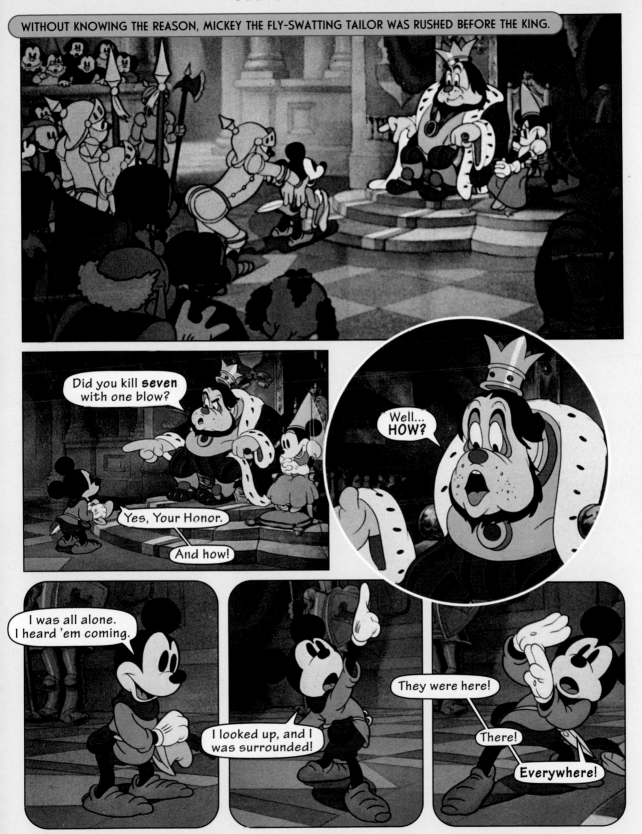

They were coming closer! The fight was on!

I swung and missed!

I missed and swung!

Yes, go on!

And then?

I swung again and again and again!!

They were right on top of me

So, I clobbered 'em.

APPLAUSE FILLED THE ROOM! THE KING WAS VERY IMPRESSED. HE ROSE . . .

BRAVO!

HOORAY!

CLAP CLAP

Brave tailor, I hereby appoint you...

ROYAL HIGH KILLER OF THE GIANT!

THE PEOPLE CHEERED AND CLAPPED WILDLY AS THE TAILOR MARCHED OUT OF THE CASTLE.

HEADING OFF TO MEET THE GIANT, THE BRAVE LITTLE TAILOR ALREADY FELT LIKE A HERO.

BRAVO!

YAY!

YIPPEE!

THAT IS, UNTIL THE DOOR SLAMMED AND HE WAS ALL ALONE. THEN HE WANTED TO GET BACK IN!

SLAM!!

BAM

BAM

BAM

YAHOO!

YIPPEE!

HOORAY!

LOOKING UP AT THE CHEERING CROWD, MICKEY SAW PRINCESS MINNIE.

Well, so long! I'll be seeing you...

I hope!

BOOM

BOOM

BOOM

Gosh... I don't know how to catch a giant.

THE GROUND SHOOK AS A HUGE SHADOW APPEARED ACROSS THE LAND—THE TAILOR RAN FOR HIS LIFE!

MICKEY RUSHED TO FIND A HIDING PLACE . . .

AS THE GIANT SAT DOWN TO REST!

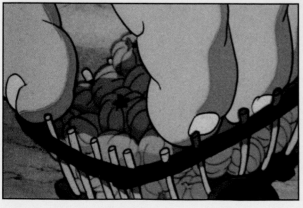

THINKING HE WAS A TASTY PUMPKIN, THE GIANT TOSSED MICKEY INTO HIS MOUTH.

PLING!

Urp! HUP-up!

THE GIANT DECIDED TO TRY TO CURE HIS HICCUPS WITH A DRINK FROM A WELL . . .

Hmmm...

EVEN IF IT MEANT PULLING UP THE ENTIRE WELL!

RRRIPPPP

MICKEY THOUGHT HE SAW A CHANCE TO ESCAPE, BUT THEN—

W-W-WHOA!

VOOOSH!

LUCKILY, MICKEY HELD ON AND WAS PULLED BACK OUT.

WOOSH!

MICKEY LANDED SAFELY ON A NICE, SOFT HAYSTACK WHERE HE QUICKLY HID, HOPING HIS TROUBLES WERE OVER.

HEY! Heh–heh–heh.

BUT THEN THE GIANT NOTICED THE HAYSTACK.

SMOKE!

Uh-oh!

HE SEARCHED FOR A LIGHT . . .

THE GIANT LEANED BACK TO ENJOY A RELAXING AFTERNOON.

SUDDENLY MICKEY AND THE GIANT WERE FACE-TO-FACE!

MICKEY SQUIRMED UP THE GIANT'S SLEEVE.

HE CUT HIS WAY OUT AND SEWED THE GIANT'S SLEEVE TIGHTLY AROUND HIS BIG HAND.

MICKEY PULLED OUT HIS TRUSTY ROPE.

ONCE AGAIN THE KINGDOM WAS SAFE! A NEW AMUSEMENT PARK OPENED . . .

WITH RIDES POWERED BY A WINDMILL AND A BIG SLEEPY GIANT WHO SNORED A LOT.

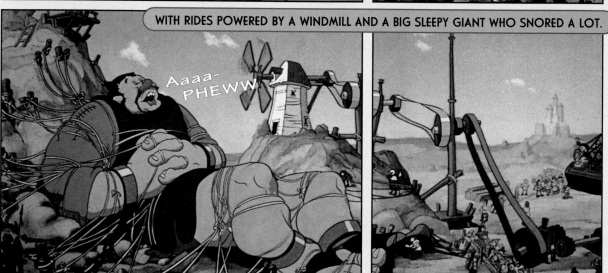

Aaaa-PHEWW

AND THE BRAVE LITTLE TAILOR MARRIED THE PRINCESS AND LIVED HAPPILY EVER AFTER.

YIPPEEE!

THE END

Mr. Mouse Takes a Trip

Premiere Date: November 1, 1940

In this traveling tale, a big nasty railroad conductor tries to keep Mickey's dog, Pluto, off a train. He underestimates Mickey's loyalty to Pluto and the ingenious tricks Mickey will use to continue the journey—but Mickey and Pluto, in turn, underestimate the conductor, who just won't quit. The contest goes first one way, then the other, but ultimately the biggest winner is the audience of this classic short film. Directed by Clyde Geronimi, previously an animator on the Disney team.

ONE

CHEERFUL DAY, MICKEY MOUSE DECIDED TO GO ON AN ADVENTURE
AND RIDE THE TRAIN FROM BURBANK TO THE NEARBY TOWN OF POMONA.

BURBANK
ELEVATION 16¾ FEET

TELEGRAMS

FREIGHT

Hey, Pluto!
Here she
comes!

AS THE TRAIN PULLED INTO THE STATION, THE ADVENTURE BEGAN!

CHUF-FA chuffa CHUF-FA chuffa

CHUF-FA chuffa CHUF-FA chuffa

SCREECH!

MICKEY AND HIS PAL RUSHED TO GET ON THE TRAIN . . .

Hurry up, Pluto!

BUT INSIDE THEY MET PETE THE CONDUCTOR, WHO WASN'T HAPPY TO SEE THEM.

HEY, YOU!

NO DOGS ALLOWED!

BLAM!

SEE?

KLUNK!

EVEN PLUTO'S LUNCHBOX WAS TOSSED ONTO THE PLATFORM.

ALL ABOARD!

Train leaving for Albuquerque! Amarillo! Azuza!

Flubbety, blubbety, blah blah blah,

AND ALL POINTS

WEST!

Huh?

MICKEY HAD AN IDEA HOW TO GET ON THE TRAIN.

ALL ABOARD!

Come on! We've gotta hurry!

RRRRIP!

M.M.

RRRRUFF!

M.M

Shhhhhh!

Oh, no!

MICKEY GRABBED THE SUITCASE AND RAN LIKE CRAZY TO CATCH THE TRAIN.

CHUF-FA chuffa

CHUF-FA chuffa

HE JUST MADE IT!

Whew!

Rruff!

Pluto, you don't want to get thrown off, do you?

Ruff! Ruff!

Be quiet, and I'll let you out.

S-T-R-E-T-C-H

POP!

Everything's okay, Pluto!

ALONG CAME PETE AGAIN.

Tickets, please!

TICKETS!

MICKEY QUICKLY REPACKED PLUTO.

TICKETS!

Uh-oh.

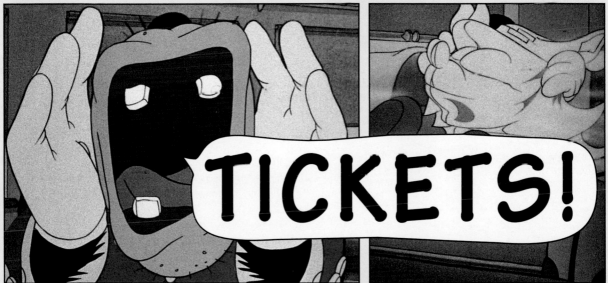

TICKETS!

HE HANDED OVER HIS TICKETS—

?

TWO OF THEM!

PETE LOOKED AT MICKEY'S SUITCASE.

Hey, you!

This baggage belongs...

UP THERE!

PLUTO WONDERED WHAT WAS GOING ON!

Rruff? Rruff?

Rruffa?

Rruffa?
Rruff?

A-ruff?
A-ruff?

IF MICKEY DIDN'T THINK FAST, PETE WAS GOING TO FIND PLUTO.

Gulp!

Ruff! Ruff!
Cough! Cough!
Rrruff! Cough!

So! It's YOU, huh?

Yeah, it's me. I guess.

All alone without your dog?

Yeah, heh-heh. All alone!

THEN HE SAW THE CONDUCTOR!

I THOUGHT SO!

MICKEY DECIDED TO SCRAM.

HEH HEH

DRAGGING PLUTO BEHIND HIM, MICKEY RAN FAST . . .

STRAIGHT INTO THE SLEEPING CAR.

PETE WAS RIGHT BEHIND . . .

A-HA!

AND HE WAS SURE HE HAD FOUND THEM.

Now I've got you!

EEEK!

WHOOPS! IT WAS A LADY!

How DARE you— you masher!

MASHER!

THWACK!

THWACK!

Take THAT! And THAT! And THAT!

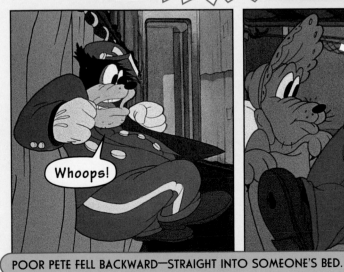

Whoops!

POOR PETE FELL BACKWARD—STRAIGHT INTO SOMEONE'S BED.

HE WAS VERY EMBARRASSED!

Oh, ex-*cuse* me. I'm so **sorry**!

You won't be disturbed again.

Huh?

Heh-heh. We fooled him.

Oh, YEAH?

PETE HAD THEM IN HIS PAWS!

JUST THEN, THE TRAIN WENT INTO A TUNNEL . . .

CHUF-FA chuffa CHUF-FA chuffa CHUF-FA chuffa

Huh?

ONCE MORE MICKEY AND PLUTO HAD ESCAPED!

HEY, YOU!

Did ya see a mutt and a little runt around here?

They went that way.

Thanks, Conductor!

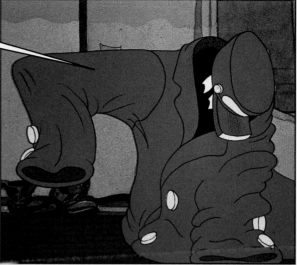

Conductor? Why, that's ME!

AND ONCE MORE PETE HAD THEM!

Shhh!

Why, you little...

PETE LUNGED—

HELP!
I'll call the conductor!

HELP!

CRASH!

AND MET THE LADY AGAIN.

Excuse me, lady.
Take it easy.

YEOWW!

CONDUCTOR!

DOINK!

A LITTLE LATER, PETE WAS STILL SEARCHING FOR MICKEY AND PLUTO . . .

OH!

I beg your pardon, Chief.

HOW!

A little papoose!

How cute!

Grrrrr

Kootchy kootchy koo!

AAARR...

EEEOW!

HE'D FOUND THEM.

Now you little...

WHIPP!

WHIPPETY-WHIPPETY-WHIPPETY

THIS TIME IT LOOKED LIKE MICKEY AND PLUTO WERE FINISHED—THEN ALL OF A SUDDEN . . .

SNAG!

ZIIIIIIING!

SNARED BY A HOOK, PLUTO WAS GOING TO BE LEFT BEHIND IF MICKEY DIDN'T DO SOMETHING FAST.

CHUF-FA chuffa CHUF-FA chuffa CHUF-FA chuffa

Now it's **your** turn!

WHOA!

KA-RASH!

Hold on, Pluto! I'll save you!

MICKEY RUSHED TO THE BACK OF THE TRAIN . . .

CHUF-FA chuffa CHUF-FA chuffa CHUF-FA chuffa

PETE FINALLY SAID GOOD-BYE TO THE TWO TROUBLEMAKERS . . .

AND THEIR SUITCASE!

WHAM!

CRASH!

Ohhhhh...

POOR MICKEY AND PLUTO—THEY WERE IN THE MIDDLE OF NOWHERE!

SOCIETY DOG SHOW

PREMIERE DATE: FEBRUARY 3, 1939

Pluto has a strong costarring role in this film, which pokes fun at high society. The plot is ingenious: As a mutt without much money or training, Pluto can't compete with the pampered and snooty dogs of the very wealthy. What he has, however, is an innately good character, as he proves when an accident turns the dog show upside down. Bill Roberts directed this tale (as well as "Brave Little Tailor"), wrapping its moral lesson in a crowd-pleasing package of action and comedy.

IT WAS THE NIGHT OF THE ANNUAL DOG SHOW. DRIVERS AND DOORMEN WERE KEPT BUSY AS THE CITY'S MOST ELEGANT OWNERS AND THEIR MOST ELEGANT DOGS BEGAN TO ARRIVE.

Welcome, madam!

ALL THE POOCHES WERE ON THEIR BEST BEHAVIOR.

The caviar had better be good!

I want a private dressing room!

BEEP BEEP!

Welcome to the Society Dog Show.

ALONG CAME A PAIR THAT WERE, WELL . . . A LITTLE DIFFERENT.

HONK HONK!

Ahhh, riff-raff!

Let's go, Pluto!

LEAVING THEIR SCOOTER AT THE CURB, MICKEY AND PLUTO MARCHED RIGHT IN!

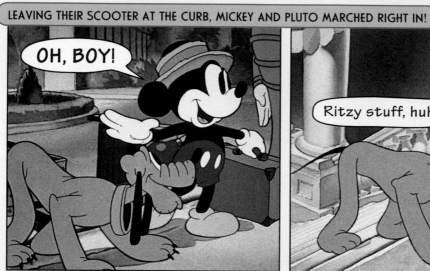

OH, BOY!

Ritzy stuff, huh?

Some place!

Gosh, Pluto, we're in...

SOCIETY!

WOW!

Up you go, champ!

13

Hey! Look at that, Pluto!

Gosh, a regular beauty shop!

What do you think of **that?** Perfume! OH, BOY!

We'll show 'em, Pluto! They ain't seen nothin' yet!

MICKEY SET UP HIS SPECIAL GROOMING TOOLS.

SWEEP!

SWEEP!

SWISH!

Oh, boy! Are you going to be handsome!

SWIPE!

WOW! I AM handsome!

AND NOW FOR THE OLD-FASHIONED HAIR DRYER.

BZZZZZZZ

AND A LITTLE PERFUME!

When I get through with you, you'll win a dozen blue ribbons!

Perfume

PUFF!

YUCK!

PUFF!

On second thought...

PUFF!

This smells TERRIFIC!

Ahhh
Ahhhh

CHOO!

But it sure does tickle!

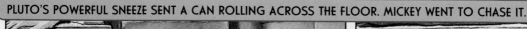

PLUTO'S POWERFUL SNEEZE SENT A CAN ROLLING ACROSS THE FLOOR. MICKEY WENT TO CHASE IT.

PLUTO WAS CHECKING OUT THE SHOW WHEN SUDDENLY . . .

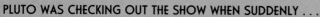

Hmm...

YOWZA!

Say, I've never seen YOU at this show before!

BOING!

I think I'm in doggie heaven.

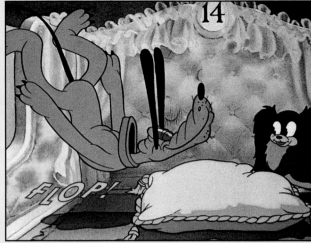

FLOP!

You're a handsome fella, aren't ya?

SMACK!

PLUTO'S NEW FRIEND WAS A PLAYFUL LITTLE PUP NAMED FIFI!

I bet you can't catch me!

Here I come!

MEANWHILE, THE JUDGE OF THE SHOW BEGAN HANDING OUT THE PRIZES.

We **deserved** to win!

Congratulations, madam!

As everyone can see... **I'M THE BEST!**

A-hem! Let's see...

Dog Number Thirteen!

Dog Number Thirteen on the judge's stand!

Number 13? That's us!

Dog Number Thirteen on the judge's stand!

PLUTO!

This is no time for women!

Dog Number Thirteen on the judge's stand!!!

Come on, Pluto...

Be dignified!

ON THE WAY TO THE JUDGE'S STAND, PLUTO STOPPED TO CHECK OUT THE MICROPHONE.

SNIFF
SNIFF

No, Pluto!
Not NOW!

SNI-I-I-FF

YANKI

WHUMP!

Of all the...

Is this a
DOG?

He's a very
fine dog, sir!
And he's
smart, too!

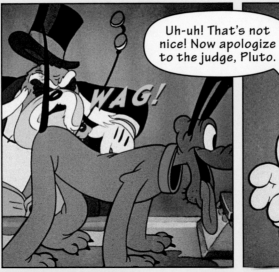

Uh-uh! That's not nice! Now apologize to the judge, Pluto.

SLURP!

Har-*rumph*!

He just wants to be **friends**, Judge!

THE JUDGE BEGAN INSPECTING PLUTO.

Come on— OPEN UP!

Hmm...

NEXT THE JUDGE TRIED TO GET PLUTO TO STAND IN THE POINT POSITION.

PLUTO TRIED, BUT HE WAS NO POINTER! THE JUDGE TOOK TOO LONG AND PLUTO STARTED TO . . .

Don't worry, Judge!

He won't—

Ah... bite.

GRRRR

Eerk!

MICKEY AND PLUTO WERE DRAGGED AWAY . . .

AND ESCORTED TO THE EXIT!

HEAVE HO!

MICKEY AND PLUTO SAT ALONE ON THE CURB.

FOR THEM, THE SHOW WAS OVER!

Don't worry, Pluto.

You're a better dog than any of them!

SUDDENLY—

ANNOUNCING THE FINAL EVENT!

An exhibition of world-famous trick dogs!

Trick dogs!?

Hey, YOU'RE a trick dog, Pluto.

A trick SKATING dog!

INSIDE THE TRICK DOGS WERE POSING FOR A PHOTOGRAPH . . .

Now, hold it!

FFFFFFLASH!

BUT THE PHOTOGRAPHER USED A LITTLE TOO MUCH FLASH POWDER, AND THE CURTAIN WENT UP IN FLAMES!

CRACKLE

CRACKLE

This looks like trouble to me!

The whole stage is catching fire!

Oh, no! I'm trapped!

CLANK!

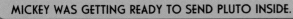

MICKEY WAS GETTING READY TO SEND PLUTO INSIDE.

Pluto, the skating marvel!

HOT DOG!

ARF!!

ARF!!

ARF!!

RUFF RUFF!

ARF!

ARF!

RUFF

GET OUT OF MY WAY!

THEY WHOLE BUILDING WAS ON FIRE!

FROM INSIDE CAME A CRY FOR HELP!

It's FIFI!

YOWLLLL!

Someone please save me!

Pluto, wait for me!

MICKEY TRIED TO FOLLOW PLUTO BUT THE FLAMES STOPPED HIM.

IT WAS UP TO PLUTO TO SAVE THE DAY!

This isn't the roller-skating rink!

74

IT WASN'T GOING TO BE EASY.

YIKES!!!

I'd better head toward that window.

Uh-oh! The window's heading toward me!

CRASH!

WHOA!!

IF ONLY SHE COULD HANG ON, PLUTO WAS ALMOST THERE!

BUT THEIR TROUBLES WEREN'T OVER YET!

ZZZZOOOOM!

UH-OH!

I hate skating on only two legs!

This could be it, folks!

Gotta keep up my speed...

Gotta aim just right...

THEY TOOK OFF FOR THE WINDOW . . .

KA-RASH!

AND FELL STRAIGHT INTO A RAIN SPOUT.

DOWN, DOWN, DOWN THEY WENT!

CLINK!

CLANK!

CLUNK!

CLINK! CLINK! CLINK!

Yikes! No brakes!

PLOP!

AROUND AND AROUND . . .

UNTIL FINALLY . . .

SPLAT!

Huh?

PLUTO!

Mickey's Delayed Date

Premiere Date: October 3, 1947

Great comedy has universal themes. Everybody—or at least the majority of men—can identify with this film, where Mickey dozes so comfortably in his armchair that he misses an appointment with Minnie. An article of clothing—Mickey's top hat—plays a surprising role in this film, but basically the plot is driven by Mickey's desire to make it up with Minnie and by his friendship with the ever-loyal Pluto. Ultimately, it's all about loyalty. Directed by Charles Nichols.

IN PLUTO'S DREAM . . .

Yum!

SLURP!

HE WAS ABOUT TO SNATCH UP AN ESPECIALLY TASTY-LOOKING BONE!

You're mine! You're MINE!

SNAP!

RRRRNNNG!

RINNNG!

Huh?

Oh!

RINNNG!

Let me talk to **Mickey!**

I'll tell **HIM** a thing or two!

Zzzzzz...

Don't bother me...

Zzzzz... Go away!

Can't you see I'm...

Zzzzz....

MICKEY!

Huh? What? Oh, hello, Minnie.

MICKEY MOUSE!

YOU'RE LATE FOR OUR DATE!

Oh, my gosh! **I forgot!**

Clothes? No problem!

Here ya go, Mickey!

No! On the BED!

Put ALL my clothes on the bed, Pluto!

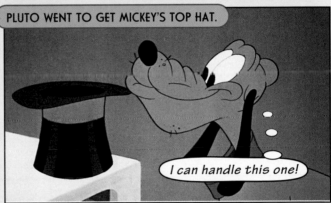

PLUTO WENT TO GET MICKEY'S TOP HAT.

I can handle this one!

Wait a minute! A hat that MOVES?

Hmmmm...

!?

BOING!

THE HAT HAD A MIND OF ITS OWN. BUT SO DID PLUTO!

So, you want to play games, huh?

UNABLE TO SEE, PLUTO STUMBLED INTO MICKEY'S CLOSET!

AT LEAST HE GOT MICKEY'S CLOTHES READY!

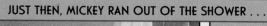

JUST THEN, MICKEY RAN OUT OF THE SHOWER . . .

Pluto! Hey!

?

WHUSH!

!

Whoa!

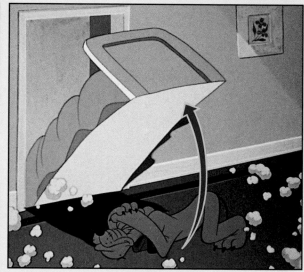

SLAM!!

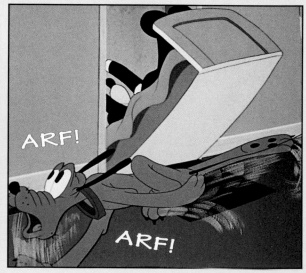

ARF!

ARF!

CRASH!

Pluto! Now look what you've—

Whaddya know!

A-hem! My **tickets**, Pluto??

Sure, Mick!

Here ya go!

OOPS! MICKEY AND PLUTO DIDN'T SEE THE TICKETS FALLING FROM THE ENVELOPE ONTO THE FLOOR!

I thank you, sir.

How do I look?

Okay?

The hat's a problem.

How's that, Pluto?

Better, huh?

PING!

Yeah! Yeah!

THE ALARM SOUNDED—NOW MICKEY WAS REALLY LATE!

Oh, my gosh!

Ruff ruff! RRuff!

Sorry, pal.

Three's a crowd... Cheerio!

MICKEY WAS FINALLY ON HIS WAY TO MEET MINNIE . . .

SOPPING WET, MICKEY GRABBED HIS HAT AND RUSHED OFF ON FOOT.

THE STREETS WERE CLEAR—BUT SURPRISES WERE EVERYWHERE!

Would someone let me out of here?

BOING!

BOING!

LUCKILY FOR MICKEY, HE FELL INTO A FREIGHT ELEVATOR AND LANDED ON A MATTRESS!

BOING!

BOING!

BOING!

AND AWAY HE RAN . . .

BEEP BEEP!

BEEP BEEP!

An hour and 15 minutes late for Minnie?

She's never going to forgive me!

HONK! HONK!

HONK!

Whoa!

WHOOOSH

Whoops!

WHILE MICKEY CHASED AFTER HIS HAT, PLUTO WAS HOME GETTING READY TO TAKE A NICE LONG NAP . . .

WHOA! THOSE WERE MICKEY'S TICKETS! PLUTO SNATCHED THEM UP AND DASHED OUT THE DOOR.

MEANWHILE, THE HAT LED MICKEY ON A MERRY CHASE!

Well...

NOTHING COULD SLOW PLUTO DOWN!

NOTHING COULD STAND IN HIS WAY!

Mickey?

KA-POWW!

THE TRASH CAN WITH MICKEY INSIDE STARTED ROLLING DOWN THE STREET!

BLAM!

IT KEPT ROLLING ALONG . . .

UNTIL FINALLY IT STOPPED!

KER-SLAM!

Uhhh...

Ahhh... HUH??

Eeee...

SO MICKEY FINALLY WENT INTO THE DANCE WITH MINNIE—ON THEIR DELAYED DATE!

THE END

MICKEY'S RIVAL

PREMIERE DATE: JUNE 20, 1936

In this Oscar-winning short, two very different villains keep the plot running at full throttle: an old flame of Minnie's, a suave playboy and prankster named Mortimer; and a large and loud bull. First Mickey competes with Mortimer for Minnie's affections, and then with the bull to save their hides—helped, it should be said, by his faithful old car. Wilfred Jackson, an early Disney studio staffer, directed the animation team that put together this delightful romp.

IT WAS A PERFECT DAY FOR A PICNIC! MINNIE PREPARED LUNCH, HUMMING A HAPPY TUNE . . .

La-de-daa da-dee-da-da.

WHILE MICKEY FETCHED THE REST OF THE FOOD FROM HIS FAITHFUL OLD JALOPY.

ALL OF A SUDDEN A SHINY NEW SPORTS CAR CAME UP THE ROAD AT A ZILLION MILES AN HOUR!

THE CAR ZOOMED RIGHT PAST MICKEY AND MINNIE AND THEN SCREETCHED TO A HALT.

Well, if it ain't my old sweetie, Minnie Mouse!

THE NEWCOMER BACKED UP HIS CAR—STRAIGHT INTO MICKEY'S JALOPY.

HE CAME STRUTTING OVER—WHAT A SMOOTH GUY!

MINNIE COULD HARDLY BELIEVE HER GOOD LUCK.

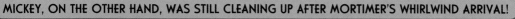

MICKEY, ON THE OTHER HAND, WAS STILL CLEANING UP AFTER MORTIMER'S WHIRLWIND ARRIVAL!

Mmfff!

Gluggg!

Phooey!

Mickey, I want you to meet Mortimer!

He's a perfect dream!

Hmph!

TA-DAA!
Thank you!
Thank you!
Thank you!

Shake, sonny!

THAT MORTIMER SURE WAS FUNNY!

BOY! HE WAS THE LIFE OF THE PARTY!

MICKEY DECIDED TO GET EVEN.

BUT ALL MICKEY GOT WAS THE SHOCK OF HIS LIFE! JUST ANOTHER ONE OF MORTIMER'S HILARIOUS JOKES.

MEANWHILE, MICKEY'S JALOPY WAS TRYING TO PUSH THAT BIG CAR OUT OF THE WAY.

RRR RRR RRRR!

VRRRRING!

WHEN HE DID, HE SAW WHAT A BIG MEAN CAR IT WAS . . .

?!?

!

HONK!

AND THE POOR LITTLE GUY GOT SCARED.

MORTIMER DID MOST OF THE EATING AT THE PICNIC, BUT MINNIE DIDN'T MIND AT ALL.

MORTIMER WAS A CLOWN, ALL RIGHT, MAKING CASTANETS OUT OF DRUMSTICKS! BUT THEN—

THEY HEARD A BULL SNORTING AWAY ON THE OTHER SIDE OF A FENCE.

SNORT SNORT

MRAURR!

GRUNT GRUNT

PAW PAW

IT WAS A **VERY LARGE BULL!**

SNORT!!!

MORTIMER SNATCHED UP THE PICNIC BLANKET . . .

For you, *señorita,* I weel fight ze bull!

Hey!

PLONK

AND BECAME A BULLFIGHTER WITH A CAPE!

AHA! Yes? No?

???

CLICKETY CLACK!

Yes! Yes!

MRAUR!

Oh, little bull-ee!

!!!

KA—

BRAVO! BRAVO!

BLAM!

Ta-daahh!

CLICKETY CLICK!

MRRROARR!

BRAVO!

TIPPETY TAP!

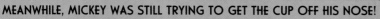

MEANWHILE, MICKEY WAS STILL TRYING TO GET THE CUP OFF HIS NOSE!

Rrrrr!

RRRRRR!

POP!

Humph!

Oh, Mickey! Isn't he wonderful?

HAH! A perfect SCREAM!

You're just jealous.

BAH!

!?

BACK AT THE BULLFIGHT . . .

Mrraur!

KA

BLAM!

MROR!

TA-DAA!

CLICKETY CLACK!

TIPPETY TAP!

CLACKETY CLACK!

BRAVO!

GRRRRR!

OH, MICKEY!

MORTIMER DECIDED THE PICNIC WAS OVER.

VRRANNNG!

BOING!

PLOP!

SCREEECH!

VRROOOOOM!

AND HE DROVE OFF AS FAST AS HE HAD ARRIVED!

WITH MORTIMER GONE THE BULL SET HIS SIGHTS ON MINNIE.

SNORT!

GRUNT!

CLOPPETY

CLOPPETY

Ah... ah...

EEK!

THE BULL CHASED MINNIE . . .

HELP!

CLOPPETY

WHILE MICKEY CHASED THE BULL.

CLOPPETY

HE CAUGHT HOLD OF THE BULL'S TAIL—AND **PU-U-U-U-ULLED!**

EERRRRRRRRK!

Uh-oh.

MICKEY WAS GETTING MAD . . .

Rrrrr...

SPLAT!

!!?!!

AARRAGGH!

CHOMP!

BUT SO WAS THE BULL! JUST AS MINNIE CAME SLIDING DOWN OUT OF THE TREE, THE BULL CHARGED!

KLNNNGG!!

THEY BARELY GOT OUT OF THE WAY!

MINNIE SLID DOWN AGAIN.

MICKEY!

MICKEY DECIDED TO TRY HIS HAND AT BULLFIGHTING

MRRRAURR!

Here, bully, bully!

Olé?

VROOOM

HE QUICKLY WRAPPED THINGS UP.
WHOOSH

WHIRL

WHUMP!

THE BULL WAS GOING TO GET MICKEY IF IT WAS THE LAST THING HE DID.

MICKEY MOVED AS FAST AS HE COULD—BUT HE WAS JUST INCHING ALONG!

MICKEY'S JALOPY SUDDENLY APPEARED!

HE WASN'T GOING TO LET THAT BULL GET MICKEY!

SO HE CHARGED AFTER THE BULL, WHO WAS CHARGING AFTER MICKEY.

HELP!

JUST AS THE BULL WAS ABOUT TO GET HIM . . .

OL' JALOPY TO THE RESCUE!!!

AND OFF HE RODE . . .

NOW THE BULL WAS **REEEEALLY** MAD!

Rrrrrrrr

MMRAUR!

Yikes!

Mickey, watch out! The bull's coming back!

Huh?

WHOA!

CLOPPETY

?

JALOPY WENT OFF AND HID AGAIN.

HI!

RATTLE RATTLE

BUT HE COULDN'T JUST LEAVE MICKEY ALL ALONE TO FACE THAT BULL.

HE COULDN'T GIVE UP—**WITHOUT A BITE!**

CHOMP!

JALOPY WAGGED HIS TAILLIGHT—AND THE BULL SAW RED!

THE CHASE WAS ON AGAIN, BUT NOW THE BULL WAS GETTING AWFULLY TIRED . . .

SNORT! GRUNT!

PANT! PANT!

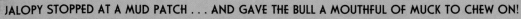

JALOPY STOPPED AT A MUD PATCH . . . AND GAVE THE BULL A MOUTHFUL OF MUCK TO CHEW ON!

SPLAT!

BLUH!

BACK IN THE TREE . . .

KRAKK!

Eeeeek!

Let's go, Minnie! LET'S GO!

EEEEEEEE!

Whoa!

JALOPY SHIFTED INTO HIGH GEAR!

PUTT PUTT

EEEBEE!

PLONK

WITH THAT OL' BULL FINALLY STUMPED, MICKEY AND MINNIE HEADED HOME.

PUTT PUTT PUTT

PUTT PUTT PUTT

So, do you still think that guy's so funny?

Who, Mortimer? NO!

SHAKE!

THE END